Bill the Warthog
MYSTERIES

QUEST
FOR THE
TEMPLE OF TRUTH

D1487958

ROSEKiDZ®

An imprint of Hendrickson Publishers Marketing, LLC.
Peabody, Massachusetts
www.HendricksonRose.com

Bill the Warthog
MYSTERIES

QUEST
FOR THE
TEMPLE OF TRUTH

Dean A. Anderson

To my wonderful wife, Mindy. She often denies she is wonderful, but she can do so no longer. It's right here in black and white.

BILL THE WARTHOG MYSTERIES: QUEST FOR THE TEMPLE OF TRUTH
©2013 by Dean Anderson

RoseKidz®
An imprint of Hendrickson Publishers Marketing, LLC.
P. O. Box 3473
Peabody, Massachusetts 01961-3473
www.HendricksonRose.com

Register your book at www. HendricksonRose.com/register and receive a free Bible Reference download.

Cover and Interior Illustrator: Dave Carleson

ISBN 10: 1-58411-079-1
ISBN 13: 978-1-58411-079-8
RoseKidz® reorder# L48304
Juvenile Fiction / Religious / Christian

Printed in the United States of America   [10]   3.2017.BRP

Table of Contents

This is kind of an embarrassing way to start off a book, but I have to admit right up front that this collection of Bill the Warthog Mysteries is the strangest of the series. And it's not just me that thinks so.

As some of you may know (but I didn't), every mystery book published is reviewed by the National Association of Mystery Editors (N.A.M.E.). The great chairman of N.A.M.E., Nathaniel Hosenfeffer himself, reviewed this very book, and he found a problem.

I guess I was working against deadlines and didn't realize that some parts of the plots in Bill's cases are suspiciously similar to plots in stories that Jesus told in the Bible. As I said, strange. Who'd link mysteries and the Bible? I mean, it's not like I took *Hound of the Baskervilles* and replaced Sherlock Holmes' name with Bill and Watson's name with Nick (and perhaps put Chris Franklin in place of the hound).

But Mr. Hosenfeffer feels strongly that you need to know. He said I could still use my stories as long as I pointed out the similarities, so I have. I hope you enjoy this book. When you solve each case along with Bill, try to guess which one of Jesus's stories matches the plot. (Just don't "borrow" like this at school.)

Dean **A**. **A**nderson

Chapter 1

The Case of the Fugitive Flyers

"How about this for a slogan – 'Not just another pretty face: Bill the Warthog, Private Investigator?'"

"I don't know, Bill," I said. "Maybe you should think it through a bit longer."

The "it" was the new flyer for my friend Bill's detective agency. I guess while I'm explaining things, I might as well tell you who I am.

My name is Nick Sayga, I'm in the sixth grade, and my best friend has tusks seven inches long.

His name is Bill, and you would never guess he was a real live warthog from Africa if you were talking to him on the phone. If you saw him in person, though, you would have no doubt.

Bill tried another slogan. "'If something smells rotten, I'll put my snout in it: Bill the Warthog.' What do you think?"

"Maybe you don't need a slogan," I said.

"All right, but which drawing do you like better, the one with the fedora and trench coat or the one with the magnifying glass?"

"I don't know about the picture, either, Bill. I think we need to emphasize the detective side of you rather than the warthog side of you."

"I will use one of the pictures. I hate to think of all that money the Thompsons spent on wart remover going to waste."

(The Thompsons are the family that took Bill in when he was young. The youngest Thompson, Shannon, took Bill from his pen at the Pottersville Zoo. The zoo didn't take good care of their animals at the time. The Thompsons treated Bill like a son and introduced him to detectives in books, like Sherlock Holmes and G.K. Chesterton's Father Brown.)

We finally finished the flyers, and it was time to hand them out. I asked a couple friends of mine, Tommy Hendricks and Hurley Smith, to help hand out the flyers in nearby neighborhoods. We left some

flyers on doorsteps, tucked some under windshield wipers, and handed some to people directly. We all met back at Merlin's Pizza Parlor when we were done. (If you're curious, we all had our own pizzas. Pepperoni for me, Hawaiian for Tommy, vegetarian without cheese for Hurley, and for Bill a special with crickets and Bermuda grass that Marty, the owner and manager, always keeps on hand for his only warthog customer.)

"Do you think your flyers will generate any business?" Hurley asked Bill while we waited for the pizzas.

"Time will tell," Bill said. "But the office answering machine may tell as well. After we finish up here, I'll check to see if I've gotten any responses."

"And I was wondering, Bill," I said. "Should I cross back over the area we covered and make sure our flyers didn't blow out into the street or lawns?"

"Good thinking," Bill said. "Littering isn't the image Warthog Investigations wants to present to the city."

Tommy went with me. Along the way we saw a couple of little kids playing with a paper airplane they had made from a flyer. We found a few crumpled flyers in the street. I picked them up and went to

throw them away in the trash can in front of the Elm Street Market. I looked inside the trash can when I tossed them in. And I saw a big pile of Bill's flyers.

I asked Mr. Lopez, the manager of Elm Street Market, if he had noticed anyone dropping flyers in the trash can.

"I did notice a young man dropping a lot of paper in that can," Mr. Lopez said. "He was about so high, and he had brown hair. The thing that drew my attention was a T-shirt he wore."

"What about the shirt?" I asked.

"It read, 'What are you looking at, Stupid?'" Mr. Lopez said. "I thought it was rude."

I'm not a detective like Bill, but Mr. Lopez gave me enough clues to figure out who probably collected the flyers and threw them away. At my school, there was a kid who liked to cause trouble – a bully by the name of Chris Franklin.

The description fit Chris, down to the obnoxious T-shirt that I had seen him wearing at school the other day. And this sounded like something he might do.

Tommy went home, but I went to talk to Bill. He was in a great mood.

"I've already gotten a response to some of the

flyers. One caller wanted to know if the agency mascot could appear at their office party. And another wanted the name of the artist that drew the warthog in the trench coat," Bill said. "A couple of other calls may lead to interesting cases."

"I'm afraid we have a case of our own to deal with first, Bill," I said. I told him what I'd learned. Then Bill and I headed over to Chris Franklin's house.

Chris came to the door after we knocked. He was wearing a sweatshirt that might have been covering his obnoxious T-shirt.

"There must be a mistake, Piglet, and is it Pooh?" Chris said after I told him we suspected that he had thrown away the flyers. (One of many things that

annoyed me about Chris was that he pretended to never remember Bill's name – or my name, either.)

"About what are we mistaken?" Bill asked.

"Well, all afternoon, I was at the public library. Because of a misunderstanding with the city authorities last year, I was asked to do community service. I decided to read stories to little kids at the public library.

"I enjoyed doing that so much, I've begun to do that on my own. That's where I was today, reading to some little ones."

"What were you reading today?" Bill asked Chris.

"Today? Oh, some fairy tales by the Brothers Grimm. I read *Snow White*. You might not realize that there was a great deal of violence in the early versions of those stories. The Queen, for example, was forced to dance to death in red hot iron shoes."

"Really," said Bill. "Did you read any of the Grimms' other tales?"

"Oh, yeah," Chris said. "*The Little Mermaid* and *Pocahontas*. The kids love those things."

"One of the great things about fairy tales," said Bill, "is that though they are fiction, they have truth in them. Of course, the fairy tale you just told doesn't have truth of any kind."

How did Bill know that Chris was telling a story?

Is it possible (as the N.A.M.E. suggests) that this story is not entirely original, but taken from the Bible?

 **Turn to page 88 to find out!**

Chapter 2

The Case of the Sneezing Brother

Caleb had one powerful sneeze. Not as powerful as Bill's sneezes, because they shook the windows, but it was still strong.

And Caleb was sneezing one sneeze after another in Bill's office. Finally he was able to stop long enough to tell us his story.

"Nick, I'm sorry, it's my allergies," Caleb said.

"I assume you're allergic to these weeds," Bill said as he picked some thistles off Caleb's shirt and popped them in his mouth.

(I had already introduced Caleb Henderson to Bill. Caleb went to my school, but he was a year younger than me. His brother Connor is in my class.)

15

"Yeah, I'm allergic to weeds. *Ah, ah, choo!*"

Bill was a little close for that blast. Fortunately he always has a handkerchief handy.

"So why were you pulling weeds?" Bill asked.

"To set up for the croquet tournament . . . *Ah-choo!*"

(Caleb and Connor's dad, Clyde "Croquet" Henderson, was in charge of the county tournament. He took it over a few years ago after a landscape magazine noted that the Henderson backyard was the flattest in the tri-county area.)

"The tournament starts tomorrow," Caleb said, "So my dad asked me to pull weeds in the yard and set up the croquet course. I told him I couldn't because of my allergies."

"Which is not exactly the best explanation for your red eyes and constant nose explosions," I said.

"I said I wouldn't weed and then my brother Connor said he would do it all. Usually Connor does nothing but waste time playing video games, so Dad was surprised."

I was about to launch into a defense of video games, pointing out the importance of eye-hand coordination, or eye-toe coordination in my case.

A look from Bill told me not to bother.

"So did your brother do the work?" Bill asked.

"No. My dad gave Connor $10 in advance for the work. Connor took the money to the video arcade to play *Mayhem, U.S.A.* and left all the work undone."

(That was one video game I hated. The player just goes around robbing fast food restaurants and kicking small dogs.)

"What did your dad say?" I asked.

"My dad had gone downtown already to get the tournament T-shirts.

"I knew the work had to be done, so I did the weeding and set up the croquet course."

"Didn't your brother care about the tournament?" Bill asked.

"My brother has never been interested in croquet. He doesn't know the first thing about it."

"So why is it you're here?" Bill asked.

"Well, Mr. Warthog," Caleb said, "when my dad got back and saw all the work done, he thought Connor had done it. He wouldn't believe me when I said I had done it."

"Is your brother still at the arcade?" Bill asked.

"I guess so," Caleb said.

"All right, Nick, try to track down Connor, then

18

meet Caleb and me at his house."

Sure enough, Connor was still at the arcade. I told Connor we had to go right away to his house. I was tempted to play a round of a new game, *Outer Space Sky Dive*, but I'd told Bill I would hurry.

Bill and Caleb were on the Henderson's front porch.

After I introduced Bill to Connor, Bill got right into it.

"Connor, your brother Caleb claims that he did the weeding and set up the croquet course, and you're taking credit for his work."

"No way," Connor said, "I did it all myself. He just wants the credit for my work."

"Connor, can you explain why Caleb's allergies have flared up?"

"Maybe he rolled in the pile of weeds I pulled," Connor said.

"You mean the pile of weeds I pulled," Caleb said.

"There's a pile of weeds around here?" Bill asked, with a bit too much enthusiasm.

"Bill," I said, "solve the case, and then we can see about snacks."

"You're right, Nick," Bill said. "Now, Connor, you

claim you set up the croquet course according to the official requirements."

"Of course."

"You set up the dozen wickets?"

"What are the wickets?" I asked.

"The wire hoops the wooden balls go through," Bill said. "Now once again, Connor, did you set up all twelve wickets?"

"Yes," Connor said, "How many time do you want me to repeat it? Man, you're pigheaded. Oh, sorry."

"Now, Caleb," Bill said, "You claim you set up the course. Did you set up all four stakes?"

"I set up two stakes."

"I'm sure you did," Bill said. "Did you hear that, Mr. Henderson?"

Mr. Henderson stepped out of the front door. "I heard it all through the mail slot. Connor, you owe Caleb $10 and an apology."

Mr. Henderson invited Bill and me to come to the tournament, and I'm thinking of entering it next year. Bill thought the invitation was a nice bonus, but felt his real reward was that pile of weeds.

Unfortunately, there was a certain kind of dandelion in the pile and Bill was allergic to it. His

sneeze blew the pile of weeds all over the course. Bill and I went to work and raked up the lawn.

Mr. Henderson noticed and gave Bill and me $10 for our trouble. I told Bill that maybe we should try to earn this kind of green for cases more often, but he said U.S. currency isn't nearly as tasty as a mix of crab grass and wild oats.

How did Mr. Henderson know that Caleb had done the work rather than Connor? And what Bible story did the lazy writer rip off this time for his plot outline?

☞ Turn to page 90 to find out!

Chapter 3

The Case of the Super Bowl Booth

Now get this straight. I am in no way saying that Chris Franklin was justified in what he did. But was it surprising, when the new kid Francis Wilkerson came to our school, that Chris teased Francis about his name? Why didn't Francis go by Frank? Or F.W.? Or "New Guy" or something? When he came to Bill for help, I asked Francis about it.

"Francis is my dad's name, too. If I went by another name, it would seem like I was embarrassed by my dad, and that wouldn't be right."

"Good to meet you, and I think Francis is a fine name," said Bill, reaching out his hoof to shake Francis' hand. "So what can we do for you?"

23

"Can you figure out why no one will go with me to the Super Bowl?"

"You're going to the Super Bowl?" I said.

"Yeah," said Francis. "It's kind of a long story."

"We've got time," Bill said.

Francis told us it started with a Yu-Hu soda. Francis and his family moved to our town last January. Where they used to live, his family had always had a big Super Bowl party every year. That year, because of the move, the party wasn't going to happen.

"The NFL championship game party was a big deal, a tradition in my old town. Even when the football game itself wasn't an exciting match, we enjoyed just getting together with other people.

"Our friends would come dressed in colors of the teams playing, and there were lots of snacks, and we always had a big touch football game in the street in front of our house at half time.

"We were unpacking the day before the game, so our family watched the game alone. Mom still got lots of chips, cookies, chili, and my favorite soda, Yu-Hu."

"Say," said Bill, "wasn't Yu-Hu running some sort of contest last year?"

"That's what I'm talking about," Francis said.

24

"They had an essay contest to win tickets to the Super Bowl. You had to write something about why Yu-Hu soda and the Super Bowl went together, and I wrote something about how Yu-Hu was the only familiar friend at our Super Bowl party."

"Making for a sad sounding story," I said.

"Whatever," Francis said. "I won box seats at the Super Bowl, twenty tickets. Transportation, food and souvenirs are all included!"

"Who were you planning to take?" Bill asked.

"Well, my parents, of course," Francis said. "And my four-year-old sister. Since I won the tickets, my parents said I could ask anyone I wanted."

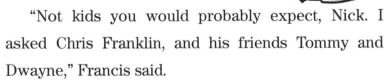

"Who did you ask that didn't want to go?" I asked.

"Not kids you would probably expect, Nick. I asked Chris Franklin, and his friends Tommy and Dwayne," Francis said.

"Why did you ask them? That bully and his friends have been picking on you since you first came to our school," I said, shocked by his choice of invites.

"That's why I asked them. They always tease me about my name sounding funny, and about being from a different place. I thought if I invited them they might stop picking on me," Francis said.

"I'm all for being kind to everyone," Bill said. "Even those who are unkind to us. But I'm not sure you thought through your motives well in this case, Francis. Still, what is it you would like us to do?"

"I was just wondering if you could find out why they said no," Francis said.

Bill agreed. We all put on our coats, caps and gloves, because it was a cold day. Well, Bill put on mittens so he didn't have to deal with the finger slots. (Bill usually buys three sets of mittens so he has a mitten for each hoof and one for the end of his tail. He never knows what to do with the spare.) We headed off to the kickball field at school where I figured we could find Chris and his friends. And they were there.

"What are you doing here, Porky and Porkette?" Chris asked in his usual classy manner.

"Oh, I love kickball fields," Bill said. "The turned-up grass often provides snacking opportunities."

"Why are you really here?" Tommy snarled.

"The usual," Bill said. "Questions."

"Then get to it," Dwayne said.

"Francis Wilkerson asked you all to watch the

Super Bowl with him. Why did you turn him down?"

"Have you ever heard him go on and on about his lame Super Bowl parties?" Chris asked. "With the stupid dressing up in team colors and NFL trivia questions and bean dip shaped like a football? We've got better things to do."

I realized they didn't understand the true nature of Francis' invitation. He must have asked them if they wanted to watch the Super Bowl with him, and they didn't realize he meant actually going to the game. I could tell by Bill's look that he knew this too, but we weren't going to let on.

"So what have you all got to do?" Bill asked.

"I told Francis my uncle is taking me deer hunting," Tommy said.

"I told him I have tickets to go to the NBA finals," Dwayne added.

"As for me," Chris said, "my grandma always takes me to the strawberry fields on the other side of town. We've been picking in those strawberry fields forever."

"Well, those are fine excuses," Bill said. "I'll assure Francis you had great reasons not to fly on the private jet in order to sit in the Yu-Hu luxury suite at the actual Super Bowl game."

As they might say on that commercial they run during the Super Bowl, the cost of a Yu-Hu soda: $1.25, the walk to the kickball field: free, the look on Chris Franklin's face: priceless.

Bill urged Francis to invite other kids to the Super Bowl. I asked him to invite my friend, Jayden Patrick, who loves football. Francis asked a lot of kids that Chris Franklin picked on, and he let Bill and me and my parents come too.

Oh, and the best part was this: at the game Bill was mistaken for a mascot, and I was mistaken for his trainer. We both got to go on the field. Some day I'll have to show you my autographed football.

In the jet on the way home I asked Bill, "Do you think Chris Franklin and his friends had as much fun in the stuff they were doing as we did at the game?"

"You mean watching the game on TV?"

"Huh?" I asked.

"Didn't you know they were lying?"

How did Bill know that Chris, Tommy and Dwayne were lying, and could this possibly be a Bible story?

 **Turn to page 92 to find out!**

Chapter 4

Phil the Warthog and the Idle Jet Pack

"Obviously, I have no problem with the talking warthog," Bill said, "but will people accept a talking chimp and aardvark as well?"

"If the situation is believable, sure," Mike said.

Mike Reed had brought another of his comic books for me and Bill to read. (Though he never said so, Mike had based Phil on Bill and he was always anxious to get Bill's opinion.) This issue's title was *Phil the Warthog: New Creatures and New Creations.*

"Besides, all respectable comic superheroes get teamed up with someone else in one book or another these days," Mike explained.

"Can I see it, guys?" I asked, reaching for the comic

in Bill's hoof. I arrived at Bill's office in the middle of this conversation, so I wanted to find out who the talking chimp and aardvark were.

The opening panels showed Phil the Warthog and his government mentor, Shady Tompkins, breaking into the labs of Dr. Werner von Doomcough. (A footnote informed new readers that Doomcough was the mad scientist who mutated Phil from an ordinary warthog into a hind-leg walking, talking super-soldier.)

SHADY: Quick, Phil, put the plastic explosives on those locks! We can't let Doomcough use these poor mutant animals for his evil schemes any longer!

PHIL: I only see two animals, that chimp and that aardvark!

SHADY: OK, Phil, set 'em free!

The next panels showed Shady and Phil leading the aardvark and the chimp out of Doomcough's labs through a series of booby traps and deadly guard posts. Finally they made it back to Shady's top secret government headquarters.

SHADY: Can you talk, little fellas?

CHIMP: Of course I can talk. Do you think Dr. Doomcough is new to the mutating animals business?

AARDVARK: I can talk as well. Thank you for

rescuing us from that terrible place.

PHIL: My name is Phil. Shady rescued me from those labs years ago. Were you ever given names?

AARDVARK: My name is Melvin and our primate friend here is Lancelot.

LANCELOT: I prefer Lance.

SHADY: Good to meet you both. I am sorry to inform you, though, that I must cut our time together short. I have a mission.

PHIL: Where are you going, Shady?

SHADY: I'm afraid that's confidential. You all will have to carry on without me for a while.

LANCE: What are we supposed to do while you're away?

SHADY: Oh, the normal heroic stuff. Protect the weak, right wrongs, you know.

PHIL: Will do, Shady!

SHADY: Oh, I just remembered. I have some tools for doing good deeds.

Shady pulled gadgets out of a big black bag.

SHADY: Phil, I want you to use these while I'm gone. These are Ultra-ears, a prototype that allows you to hear every little thing from miles away.

PHIL: Cool!

SHADY: Melvin, here is a device called Extendo-nose. It will allow you to smell danger.

MELVIN: And perhaps ants as well?

SHADY: I guess you'll find that out.

MELVIN: Awesome!

SHADY: And for you, Lance, a jet pack.

LANCE: Gee whiz. How very James Bond.

SHADY: Off I go. Do some good!

Panels showed Phil using his Ultra-ears to listen for those in danger. He heard a kitten in a tree and brought him down. He rescued men from a burning building, a woman trapped in a car at the bottom of a cliff and a boy named Timmy who had fallen in a well.

Later panels showed Melvin using his Extendo-nose to find ants. As good deeds, Melvin tracked truffles for French chefs and detected dangerous gasses and mildew in neighborhood homes.

A single panel showed Lance using the jet pack as a table to hold his blender as he made banana shakes.

The next panel showed Shady Thompkins returning in the Ultra-jet.

SHADY: So, Phil, did you use the Ultra-ears?

PHIL: You bet, Shady. They enabled me to rescue men, women, children and kittens.

SHADY: Excellent, Phil. Were you able to use the Extendo-nose, Melvin?

MELVIN: Not only did I use it to find treats; I helped further culinary excellence and domestic safety!

SHADY: I'm not sure what you mean by that, but it sounds like you did good stuff, Melvin. Lance, what did you accomplish with your jet pack?

LANCE: Me? Oh, I went up high and took pictures.

The next panel showed Lance swinging by the light fixtures to his room. He came back with some photographs of Earth taken from a high altitude.

LANCE: See, look at these amazing shots. I think they'll be useful.

SHADY: Interesting photos. These appear to have been taken from about 70,000 feet. Quite interesting. You didn't take them.

PHIL: Can't the jet pack go that high?

SHADY: Of course the jet pack can.

PHIL: Do the photos themselves give some indication they were taken by someone else?

SHADY: No, but they obviously were. Lance, why didn't you use the jet pack?

LANCE: Because I was afraid what you would do with me if I broke it. I know Dr. Doomcough would have punished me mightily if I hurt one of his toys.

SHADY: You think so, Lance? Phil, you may have the jet pack. Put it to good use. Lance, if you can see no difference between me and Doomcough, you can return to him.

LANCE: OK, I will.

The next panels showed Lance going out the door and down the road. Shady ordered Phil to follow Lance with the jet pack to see where he went, and that was the end of the comic.

"I like it, Mike," I said. "I wonder how Shady knew Lance was lying. And that story seems familiar. Did you get it from somewhere?"

"Sorry, Nick, no time to answer," Mike said. "I've got homework."

"Bill?"

"Sorry, Nick, I've got paperwork."

How did Shady know Lance was lying? And from what part of the Bible does the comic's story come?

 **Turn to page 94 to find out!**

Chapter 5

The Case of the Bogus Bowler

"Sure, the shoes are cool," said Bill. "But I don't understand the attraction of bowling, Nick."

"The Elm Bowl Bowlathon is a big deal," I explained. "They cover it on ESPN 4. And how many bowling tournaments let kids roll alongside adults?"

Our conversation was interrupted by a knock at Bill's office door. It was Brian Samples.

Brian was in his wheelchair, of course. I guess it's not "of course" to you because you don't know him. But as far as I know, Brian has always been in a wheelchair.

Brian does lots of stuff anyway. He's good at video games. (Not as good as me, but who is?) He also is good at things you wouldn't expect. He joins us sometimes for Ultimate Frisbee. He plays basketball at our school and was in a wheelchair rugby league. The thing he's really good at is bowling.

"Chris Franklin is trying to get me kicked out of the Elm Bowl Bowlathon," Brian told us. Bill and I wanted to hear more.

Brian explained, "To get into the Bowlathon, you have to have a qualifying game at the Elm Bowl. You know the bowling alley on Elm Street?"

"I'm familiar with it," Bill assured him.

"To qualify, you have to score at least seven strikes or spares in a game. A strike is when you knock down all the pins with one ball, and a spare is when you knock down all the pins with two balls."

"I'm familiar with the terms, Brian," Bill said.

"I'm sorry," Brian said. "I just didn't know if warthogs could bowl."

"I never have," Bill said. "I've been reading about the game because of the Bowlathon."

"OK. Anyway," Brian continued, "I threw a game with five strikes and three spares. I took my scorecard to the manager, who sent it in to qualify my game for the Bowlathon."

"Congratulations," I said.

"Non-congratulations. Chris Franklin sent this picture to the Bowlathon chairman," Brian said as he handed me a photograph.

It showed a foot in a bowling alley crossing a line.

"I don't get it," I said.

"That's my foot," said Brian. "Above the foul line. Chris said I was cheating, going over the foul line."

"I still don't get it," I said.

"You're not supposed to go over the line. But the rules I've always played by with my friends is that my wheels won't go over the line. I've never worried about my foot going over the line."

"According to the rules, it is a violation if the player's foot crosses the line. But perhaps you could talk to the officials," Bill said.

"Could you talk to Chris Franklin first?" Brian asked.

"Sure," said Bill.

We found Chris with his friend Dwayne at Elm Bowl.

"Hey, Chris," I said. "I didn't know you could bowl."

"If it isn't Sherlock Piglock and that guy that hangs out with Sherlock Piglock."

"Your wit continues to scintillate," Bill said.

"Scina what?" Dwayne asked.

"When did you start bowling?" I asked Chris.

"Just last week," he said. "I catch on to any sport real quick. There are only so many Bowlathon slots for those under sixteen and I got one of the slots. I had a game with eight spares."

"Are those bumpers on your lane?" Bill asked.

I hadn't noticed, but Chris did have the bumpers up. Bumpers are barriers to keep the bowling ball from going into the gutter on either side of the lane.

"Oh, yeah," Chris said. "The kids who were playing this lane before us had the bumpers up, and the management was too busy to take them down."

"So Chris," Bill said, "You've become a bowling expert. Could you help me figure out the game?"

"Always happy to help the ignorant," Chris said.

"If you knock down ten pins with one ball . . ."

"That's a strike," Chris said.

"And that's worth how many points?" Bill asked.

"Ten points," Chris said.

"And if you roll ten of those strikes worth ten points in a row, how many points is that?" Bill asked.

"Are you as dumb in math as you are in bowling? One hundred points," Chris said.

"Thanks for your help," Bill said.

"Any time, Hoglock Homeboy," Chris quipped.

"Where are we going now?" I asked Bill as we headed out of the bowling alley.

"To see Felix Grumley, the chairman of the Bowlathon."

The Grumley Estate was a big place. An older gentleman answered the door and said he was Mr. Grumley. "Good to meet you, young men," he said.

"Good to meet you as well," Bill said.

Mr. Grumley gave Bill a good looking over. "I never know what style you young people will come up with next."

"We're here to talk about the Bowlathon," Bill said.

"Well, I'm afraid we're out of spots for the under-sixteen bracket."

"Nick and I aren't looking to bowl, but we wanted to talk to you about a couple of the other bowlers. Did you receive this photo in the mail?"

Mr. Grumley looked over the picture of Brian Samples's foot. "Yes, I did get this picture in the mail. The wearer of this shoe was over the foul line."

"Did you know, Mr. Grumley, that the foot in that

picture belongs to Brian Samples, a very good bowler who happens to be in a wheelchair?"

"I didn't know," Mr. Grumley said.

"And did you know that the picture was sent to you by Chris Franklin?" Bill asked.

"Chris Franklin? I granted him an exemption to enter the Bowlathon. He said he had to qualify using a game with the bumpers stuck in place. He complained about a boy in a wheelchair going over the line?"

Mr. Grumley was so upset that Chris had squealed on Brian that he banned Chris from the Bowlathon for five years. Brian was allowed to bowl and did well.

The next week, Bill and I went bowling. Bill rolled the ball with his tusks and he did OK. I could tell he was bothered by something, though.

"Nick, I never did get to use my evidence against Chris to prove he didn't know about bowling."

What evidence did Bill have that Chris didn't know about bowling? And what evidence is there that this story is from the Bible as well?

 Turn to page 96 to find out!

Chapter 6

Bill the Warthog
Goes to the Dogs

When my mom and I took our dog, Daisy, to the Mighty Mutts Dog Show, we hoped she would do well. We didn't expect Bill to take the prize.

Some of you may remember me talking about Daisy. There was some mystery about how we got her, which Bill helped to clear up.

The embarrassing thing is when I talked about that, I described how important it is for kids to give new pets lots of attention when they get them. But after we got Daisy, I spent a lot of time with Bill, so Daisy ended up getting her attention from my mom.

Mom really liked to take Daisy for walks, and Mom started to train her. Daisy can do amazing tricks –

speak, beg, play dead, pretend to pray and dance ballet. Mom taught her all this stuff.

Max "Arf" Stevenson was coming to town. Max hosts *Mind over Mutts*, that show on the Doggie Channel that gives obedience training tips. He's been going around the country hosting dog shows, so we knew we had to enter Daisy in the competition.

A lot of shows are for purebred dogs. Max's show was only for mutts, or mixed-breed dogs. There were awards in three categories: best looking mutt, most unusual looking mutt and most obedient mutt.

We hoped Daisy would win in the obedience category.

The event was at the convention center in town. Bill asked if he could come along and my mom said he could.

I warned Bill there might be some slow patches, so he brought his briefcase of paperwork and I brought my backpack with homework. I helped pack for Daisy, too. I put her leash, some cans of dog food and a can opener in my backpack, and I put Daisy's doggie biscuits in my mom's purse.

The dog biscuits were especially important. In a compulsory part of the obedience competition, the

dogs would have to balance biscuits on their noses until their masters signaled them to toss the biscuits in the air and eat them.

When we got inside the convention center, there were a lot of people in the stands and a lot of dogs and people on the  main floor. You had to register for one of the three competitions, so Mom signed Daisy up for the obedience competition. We stored the backpack, briefcase and Mom's purse in a cupboard in a backstage area.

The best looking and most unusual looking mutt competitions were first. Each section was narrowed down to ten dogs per category. Mom was thrilled when Daisy was named as one of the ten finalists in the obedience competition.

I thought then it would be time for the finals, but Max "Arf" wasn't there yet. The people running the competition announced that his flight had been delayed, and we might need to wait a couple of hours.

I was surprised Bill and I didn't get bored as we waited. It was fun to go around and watch the dogs, especially the ones working on their tricks. I saw a poodle/beagle mix that could hop on one foot and a St. Bernard/malamute mix that could tackle a guy in full football gear.

I was glad I had brought the dog food for Daisy, because she got hungry. So did a lot of the other dogs, and I saw some of the people feeding their dogs the biscuits that were going to be needed for the obedience finals. When I went to get a can of dog food from my backpack, I noticed a tall blond woman hurriedly leaving the backstage room, but I didn't think anything of it at the time.

Finally, they announced that Max "Arf" was on his way and would arrive in ten minutes. It was then that some of the people in the obedience competition began to realize their mistake in using up their dog biscuits and began scrambling to get more. Unfortunately, there weren't any stores open near the convention center.

I went to get the dog biscuits from my mom's purse, but they were gone. Then I remembered the woman I had seen near our stuff earlier. I went to talk to Bill.

Bill went to talk the woman I had seen earlier. Her name was Mrs. Emily Thornton Bilencheck, and she had a big brown dog that looked like no dog I had ever seen. She had told the judges Cujo was a mix of at least a dozen breeds.

She also held in her hands a bag of Happy Pup doggie biscuits, the brand we had brought.

She was surprised when Bill spoke (I had the feeling she thought Bill was one of the contestants), but she did answer his questions.

"My friend Nick says you were looking in his cupboard. Were you?" Bill asked.

"I believe I did," said Mrs. Bilencheck. "But I immediately saw it was not mine, and I moved along."

"That is the same brand of dog biscuits that Daisy eats," Bill said.

"I'm sure this is some misunderstanding," Mrs. Bilencheck said. "Perhaps Nick's mother took the biscuits out of her purse when she was looking for car keys at home. I do the same kind of thing all the time."

"Mrs. Bilencheck, your remarks prove those aren't your dog biscuits. I'm afraid I have to admit that I recorded your voice without permission, but Max 'Arf' will be interested in listening to what you said."

"Whatever do you mean?" Mrs. Bilencheck asked.

Bill took her aside and said something to her, but I

didn't hear what. Then Mrs. Bilencheck gave me the doggie biscuits, and I brought them to my mom.

Turned out five of the ten finalists in the obedience contest didn't have the doggie biscuits when Max "Arf" Stevenson arrived.

Daisy did very well with the required events (including the biscuit on her nose) and Max "Arf" seemed very impressed with her ballet. Mom was thrilled when she got second place and didn't mind that Daisy lost to Putty-kins, the football-playing mutt.

The biggest surprise was Bill's first place win in the most unusual-looking mutt competition. Of course, Bill had to turn down the prize, even though it meant embarrassing the judges and losing out on a year's supply of Happy Pup doggie treats. When they found out he saved them from the incident with Mrs. Bilencheck, the judges gave Bill five boxes.

How did Bill know Mrs. Bilencheck had taken the doggie biscuits? And where is this storyline stolen from the Bible?

 **Turn to page 98 to find out!**

Chapter 7

The Case of the Stashed Treasure

"Avast, me mateys, how be ye scurvy dogs?"

I had no idea what my friend Seth Austin was saying, but Bill apparently did. (Bill had solved a case for Seth before. Perhaps you read "The Case of the Nose Job.")

"We be well, me hearty, but Talk like a Pirate Day be next week, not today," Bill said.

"I know," Seth said. "But I've got to start practicing now. You see, I will be the treasure hunter this year."

As you may know, September 19 is International Talk like a Pirate Day. But my town is the only place I know of that makes a big deal about it.

There is a town picnic where everyone is supposed

to dress like a pirate. There's lots of food and music. We play games like "Pin the Eye Patch on the Pirate's Parrot" and "Plastic Sword Fight on the Plank."

The highlight is the big treasure hunt. One kid is chosen by a drawing to search for 10 gold doubloons. Now, I knew that this year's kid was Seth.

"So what can we do for you?" Bill asked.

"Well, Bill," Seth said, "I was wondering if you could be a part of my crew."

Every kid chosen for the hunt was allowed to pick two crew members. The hunt had different sections. One crew member could actually physically join in on part of the hunt, and one other could give one bit of advice in another part of the treasure hunt.

"I'd be glad to help anyway I can, matey," Bill said.

It takes a bit of getting used to, seeing a warthog wearing a trench coat and fedora. That is nothing compared to seeing Bill dressed as a pirate.

I met up with Bill at the Talk like a Pirate picnic at the Elm Street Park. He was wearing red and orange striped pants, a ruffled white shirt with a red vest, an eye patch and a hook for a hand.

"I tried to wear a peg leg," he said, "but I have a hard enough time walking on two legs as it is."

There was lots of food, though I don't think it was particularly pirate food: barbecued chicken, potato salad, biscuits, Jell-O and pies. I guess the chocolate coins were piratey.

Then there were the games everyone could join in on. I came in fifth in the booty sack race, but at least I beat Chris Franklin. Bill entered the Pin the Eye Patch on the Pirate's Parrot competition and accidentally pinned the patch on Principal Kingstone's back.

Then it was time for Seth's big treasure hunt. He had an hour to find the coins in three stages in three locations.

The first stage was in the park pool. The second stage was on the soccer field. The third stage was in the ranger's office. I thought the office would be the easiest stage.

A couple hundred people were gathered around the pool. There were miniature ships floating in the water, along with toy sharks. At the bottom of the pool were sunken ships and treasure chests. Five coins were hidden in the pool.

There was so much stuff in the pool, I thought Seth would need the full hour to find those five coins, especially the way the officials had Seth dressed.

Besides dressing him in a pirate hat, shirt and pants, they tied one of Seth's legs back and gave him a peg leg to wear.

Seth had asked his sister, Paige, to help with this stage. Paige was a great swimmer. She was wearing a swimsuit, flippers and goggles.

While Seth used a net to scoop the floating objects, his sister Paige dove down in the pool to hunt. Seth quickly found the first doubloon taped to the bottom of a shark and another attached to a ship. Paige found three coins at the pool bottom.

The pool only took about ten minutes, and Seth rushed to the soccer field. I didn't see how he would find the coins, but Seth had stashed a rake.

The judges didn't object to the rake. It still took Seth half an hour to find the next four coins. When Seth got to the ranger's office, there were only about fifteen minutes left.

It was starting to get dark when Seth rushed in. The office looked kind of cool – they had decorated the outside like an old time pirate jail. It looked, though, like they had emptied the inside of the office.

Seth came out after ten minutes and called to Bill for advice.

"Bill, I don't know what to do. There's nothing in that office. It's not that big, and I've searched the whole place."

"Are you sure, Seth?" Bill asked. "Is the office completely empty?"

"Well, I can't see real well in there. The lights won't

 go on, and the only thing they left inside is a stupid flashlight that doesn't work. But I felt around all the walls and floor and even the ceiling. There's nothing there!"

"May I have a minute to think?" Bill asked.

"There are only two minutes left!" Seth shouted. "But OK, just one minute."

Bill sat down. I watched my watch. After 40 seconds Bill grinned.

"I think he's got it," I said to Seth.

Seth went to Bill, who whispered in his ear. Seth rushed into the office and came out with the coin.

Everyone cheered. You see, the treasure hunters get to keep every coin they find. If Seth had only gotten nine gold coins, that would be pretty good.

Get all ten coins, and you win the key to the city. For the rest of the year, different stores throughout town will donate treats to the winner.

No one had found all ten coins for years. Now pizza and ice cream parlors, hamburger and hot dog stands, and even the video arcade will grant Seth various goodies for the year to come.

All Bill asked for was crickets from the pet store.

Seth's winning made everyone in town happy. (Except maybe Chris Franklin. Last year when he was the treasure hunter, Chris found only two coins.)

I did wonder where that tenth coin had been.

Where was that tenth coin? And what Bible story was "borrowed" here?

 Turn to page 100 to find out!

Chapter 8

The Case of the Film Fake

"Now see, here is another disappointing title. *Hog Tied* has nothing to do with hogs, let alone warthogs. It's just an old western," Bill continued his mini-tirade. "Besides that animated film about lions, you never see warthogs featured prominently in films. By the way, I think the lion film would have been much improved if it had been *The Warthog King*."

"So what kind of film would you make about warthogs?" I asked.

"Glad you asked, Nick," Bill said. "How about this? A documentary titled *March of the Warthogs*! Box office gold, I tell you."

Fortunately, Mr. Lang, the manager of Fritz's

Family Videos, came out to meet us before I had to hear Bill tell me that studios should get to work on *Raiders of the Lost Warthog* or *The Hogfather*.

"So you really are a warthog. I thought that picture was just an advertising logo," said Mr. Lang. "Well, whatever you are, since you're here, let me tell you my problem. It has to do with an employee."

It seemed Mr. Lang had made a most unfortunate hiring. "His name is Pauly Short, and I hired him as a sales clerk because he claimed he was an expert on films. He said he went to film school and knew all about the history of cinema."

"So what's been the problem?" Bill asked.

"Well, he doesn't really work during his shifts," Mr. Lang said. "He just sits around and watches movies. Also, I think he lets friends check out films without paying for them. But I was so excited to hire him initially that I gave him a year-long contract."

"So if you fired Pauly, you'd have to pay him for the whole year?" I asked.

"Sadly, so," said Mr. Lang.

"Unless perhaps you could prove that he was not truthful in his application for the job," Bill said. "And I assume that is why you called us."

"Exactly," said Mr. Lang.

Mr. Lang told us when Pauly would be working next, and we agreed to come back to the store then.

Bill told me we wouldn't approach Pauly (who was working at the front counter) directly until after we took time to observe him at work. Fritz's Family Videos no longer had many videotapes, but instead has mainly DVDs and video games. Bill wandered the DVD aisles while I went to the gaming section. (I had been waiting for a chance to look at *Electronic Gaming Power* because it had an article with tips for that new racing game, *Grandma's Driving School*.)

We both listened as Pauly made one strange phone call after another.

"Hello, yeah, I know you're Merlin's Pizza. Can I talk to Marty, please? Hey, Marty, this is Pauly from the video store. I just noticed  you've had this *Swimming the Sauces of Italy* documentary out for over two weeks. Don't worry about paying the late fees, dude, I'm taking them off the system right now. Just bring the DVD in by the end of the day, and I may give you a certificate for a free rental. Once again, this was Pauly, Pauly Short."

Bill and I listened to Pauly make calls like that to Mr. Grumley at the bowling alley, Mr. Lopez at the market and a bunch of other people, promising all of them that he'd cancel late fees or give them free rentals.

Eventually, Bill intervened.

"Excuse me, could you help me find a movie?"

"Sure, I'm kind of an expert. What are you looking for?" Pauly asked as he turned toward us. Then he looked at Bill. "Say, are you going to some kind of costume party? Am I on one of those prank TV shows?"

"No," Bill said. "This is no costume. I wear a trench coat and fedora all the time. The film I'm looking for is set in ancient times. It is called 'Ben' something-or-other."

"Oh, yeah. Here it is," Pauly said after he searched for the title on the computer. "You're looking for *Ben Hur*. We have the 1925 version and the 1959 version."

"I believe I want the 1925 version. Have you seen it?" Bill asked.

"Well, yeah," Pauly said. "I'm quite the film buff. I've seen all the classics."

"Then you have certainly seen the 1925 *Ben Hur*. That actor who played Ben Hur – I believe it was Ramon Novarro," Bill said.

Pauly looked at his computer and said confidently, "Of course, Charlton Heston played Ben Hur in the 1959 version."

"But I prefer Novarro," Bill said. "He had such a commanding voice."

"Oh yeah, for sure," Pauly agreed.

"And the cinematography was wonderful. The colors were so vibrant with the Romans' red robes against the blue skies behind the green hills. There is such wonderful color throughout the whole film, especially in the chariot race," Bill said. He really seemed to be getting into this.

"Totally, dude," Pauly nodded.

"Besides the chariot race," Bill said, "my favorite part was when you agreed to tender your resignation to Mr. Lang because you lied on your application."

Pauly seemed shocked, but Bill talked quietly to him.

"Somehow, I knew this was coming," Pauly said.

"Is that why you were making those phone calls?" Bill asked.

"For sure, man," Pauly said. "So, like, if I go to those other places for jobs, they'll remember me as the dude who was so helpful at the video store."

As we walked back to Bill's office, he said, "You know, though I disapprove of Pauly's dishonesty, I must admire his foresight. He probably will find a new job, and I hope this time he works with integrity."

"I'm just thinking about what I'll do with my free game rentals from Mr. Lang," I said.

"Have you ever wondered," Bill said, "why they don't have more video games featuring warthogs? Like *Pac-Hog* or *Aardvark-tomb Raider* or . . ."

How did Bill prove Pauly lied on his application? And is this story as much of a remake as the 1959 *Ben Hur*, re-scripted from the Bible?

 ☞ **Turn to page 102 to find out!**

Chapter 9

The Case where Bill Goes Wild

I was telling Bill about a nightmare I had. You might have had a dream like this, too. In it I found myself at school in just my underwear.

Bill said he had a dream that was worse, but I'll let him tell you about it. Here it is:

I dreamed I was wearing my suit, trench coat, fedora and patent leather shoes, which was very embarrassing because I was the only warthog who was clothed.

I dreamed I was in South Africa, the country my family comes from, and I was with a sounder of warthogs. (A group of warthogs is called a "sounder.")

Anyway, the other warthogs were all staring at me.

I tried to talk to them, but they didn't speak English, and I didn't speak warthog.

There were several adult female warthogs, and several young ones. And one adult male warthog that didn't seem happy to have me there. He approached me and seemed to want to butt heads.

So I did the sensible thing, and ran away. But as I looked beyond the sounder, I saw a glint of light by a baobab tree. I decided to circle around and see what it was.

It seemed to take forever, but I finally made it around behind the place where I saw that glint. It was a hunter with a scope, aiming at the sounder of warthogs. The poacher was about to fire his rifle.

Without thinking, I got down on all fours and ran forward, using my tusks on the poacher's, um, rearmost region. He went down. Still holding onto his rifle, he got up and went running to his Jeep, and off he drove.

I noticed a bumper sticker on the Jeep which read, "Property of the No Worries Inn."

I knew in the dream where the game ranger lived, so I went to see him. I knocked on his door. He didn't answer.

I went around the house and could see he was in a sitting room watching TV. So I knocked on the door again. And again, and again, until he finally answered.

"Are you the game ranger?" I asked.

"Yes, I am Game Ranger Deman," he said. "But I don't have time for you now; I'm watching my stories on the telly."

"There was a poacher out on the savannah who was about to shoot at a sounder of warthogs!"

"What do I care about warthogs?" Deman asked. "Tourists come to see lions and elephants and giraffes. They don't care about warthogs!" And with that he went back inside, slamming the door.

Well, I couldn't let this man rest, knowing my relatives were in danger. All day long I kept knocking at the door. I stood outside his window and called and called.

I even grunted outside his window. I did my best imitations of lions and hyenas and elephants. What finally did the trick was convincing a bunch of gnus to stage a stampede outside his house, knocking over his clothesline.

Out of the door he came, saying, "All right, warthog, where is this alleged poacher?"

At the No Worries Inn, I described the man I had seen to the desk clerk. He said it sounded like a man by the name of Eggleston who had rented one of the hotel jeeps. The clerk called his room and soon Eggleston came down to the lobby. He was the same man I had seen with the rifle.

It did not take long for the man to deny the charges.

"This is the most absurd thing I have ever heard," said Eggleston. "Yes, I was out on the savannah today, but why would I want to kill warthogs?"

"Might be one of many reasons," said Game Ranger Deman. "There are people who kill warthogs and stuff them and bring them home as a sick kind of prize. There are places where one can get good money for the tusks, from people who believe the tusks can be ground up for medicine.

"And another reason," said the game ranger, looking at me, "Might be because warthogs are downright annoying."

"Oh, I don't find them annoying," said Eggleston. "In fact, I'm here to study them. Yes, that's it. I'm not some phony big game hunter just here to bag my prize and go home. I am here to study the creatures."

"What aspect of warthog life are you here to study?" I asked.

"Oh, I've been preparing for a prolonged study," said Eggleston. "I want to study how the seasons affect warthogs. So you see, I plan to come in December to see how they live during the chillier time of year and come in June to see how they live during the warmer season."

"Oh, really," I said.

"Yes," said Eggleston. "I'm sure you know that  warthogs often can be found in abandoned aardvark burrows. Well, it is my theory that they insulate those burrows for warmth in the cool season."

"Such as December, January and February," I said.

"Now you're getting the idea," he said.

"Are you from the United States?" I asked Eggleston.

"Yes," he said, "I suppose my accent gave me away. Really, I have been researching for years to prepare myself for this field-study of warthogs."

"If you will please excuse me and Game Ranger Deman for a moment," I said.

In the dream, I spoke to the game ranger. Soon Eggleston was under arrest and the warthogs of the wild were a bit safer for a time.

"Well, that was quite a dream," I said to Bill. "I don't understand how you were able to prove to the game ranger that you were telling the truth and Eggleston wasn't."

"Oh, the evidence was all there in what Eggleston said. The game ranger would have to do his job. I just hope for my kinspigs' sakes that the real game rangers in Africa are more diligent than the one in my dream."

What did Eggleston say that gave him away? And surely this story can't be found in the Bible, can it?

 Turn to page 104 to find out!

The Case of the Unwanted Gift

"Mr. Warthog, you've got to stop my brother from buying me a birthday present."

This was the unusual request Madison Brady made of Bill after knocking on his office door.

"What is Tyler trying to give you?" I asked. "A pinch to grow an inch? A sock to grow a block?"

"Nothing like that, Nick. He's trying to give me something nice."

"I'm really having a hard time seeing your problem, um, miss," Bill said.

"Oh, I'm sorry, Bill," I said. "This is Madison Brady, Tyler Brady's younger sister. I've told you about Tyler. Remember the baseball trading card fanatic?"

"I do remember," Bill said.

Tyler is as crazy about baseball cards as I am about video games, which means very, very crazy.

"So, Madison," Bill said, "What is your problem? Is Tyler getting you something you don't like?"

"No. He wants to buy me something very cool: a vintage Lucy Bell camper trailer pulled by a Lucy Bell Corvette."

"Oh, I see the problem," Bill said. "You're obviously too young to drive a car, so you think this would be a foolish purchase."

"It's not a real car," Madison said. "It's accessories to go with my Lucy Bell dolls. The problem is that Tyler wants to buy the toy at Zimmerman's Antiques."

"Now I think I'm beginning to see the problem, Bill," I said. "The Zimmermans overcharge on everything, selling antiques to tourists."

"That's part of it," Madison said. "This toy is considered a classic from the 1970s, so they're charging a hundred dollars for it. But it's a bit banged up, so that's probably twice what the toy is worth."

"What else is bothering you, Madison?" Bill asked.

"The other thing that's bothering me is that he's selling everything he has to pay for this present."

"When you say everything, you mean, everything?" I asked.

"Everything he can get money for. He sold his video game system along with the baseball video games to our neighbor, Bobby," she said.

("Why didn't he sell it to me?" I thought, but didn't say so out loud.)

"He sold his mitt, bats and baseballs to Replay Sports. When I left, Tyler was on his way to Stanley's Comics and Cards with his baseball trading card collection," Madison said.

"He is actually going to sell his cards?" I said. "Bill, Madison's right, something fishy is going on. Madison, I don't think you need a detective. Your brother needs a psychiatrist!"

"Maybe we could talk to your brother," Bill said. "We might catch him at Stanley's. Let's go."

We met Tyler as he was on his way out of the Comics and Cards store.

"You didn't go through with it, did you, Tyler?" Madison asked.

"You bet I did. I have got enough money now to buy the Lucy Bell camper trailer. Sorry you'll already know what I'm getting you a week ahead of time."

"Tyler, I appreciate you thinking about me, but I'm afraid you'll regret selling your cards and then blame me."

"It's my decision," Tyler said.

He looked at Bill and me. "What are you two doing here? I take it you're Nick's, um, friend."

"Bill the Warthog," Bill said. "Pleased to meet you, Tyler. Madison hoped we might talk you out of doing anything rash."

"I don't think you'll talk me out of anything. You can come with me to Zimmerman's Antiques, though, all of you."

Zimmerman's Antiques mainly has a lot of old furniture. They have a corner with kids' stuff. They even have some old computers and video game systems, but it always costs more than I'd want to pay.

"Well, here it is," Tyler said, "The Lucy Bell camper trailer with the Lucy Bell Corvette."

"Tyler," Bill said, "this is your decision, but it does seem to us to be a rather absurd choice, since your sister is against your buying this present."

"I know, Mr. Warthog, this seems like a strange choice but you can't just look on the outside. Sometimes you really have to look on the inside."

Bill picked up the toy and looked it over. "I see what you mean," he said. Bill then went across the room to examine a collection of porcelain pigs.

Madison and I tried a while longer to persuade Tyler, but nothing doing.

He brought the Lucy Bell toy and his money to Mr. Zimmerman at the cash register.

"Well," Mr. Zimmerman said, "I'm rather surprised to find a boy buying this toy."

"It's for my sister," Tyler said.

"Well, that's nice," Mr. Zimmerman said.

Usually the only interaction I'd had with the owner of the store was when he was yelling at me to not touch something. I'd only seen a mean expression on his face. Now his expression was different, kind of, well, almost kind.

"I shouldn't mention this, young man," he said, "But we're going to have a sale on toys next weekend. You might want to wait until then to buy this."

"But someone else could buy it by then, right?"

"I suppose so," said the man.

"Then I'm not taking that chance," Tyler said. "I'm buying it now."

So a few minutes later we were all heading out of the store, Tyler holding a stupid old girl toy that his sister didn't seem excited about.

"So, are we going back to Stanley's Comics and Cards?" Bill asked.

"Of course," Tyler said. "At least for an estimate."

"What are you both talking about?" Madison asked.

"Perhaps you could use this," Bill said, pulling a Swiss army knife out of his trench coat pocket.

Tyler sat on a bus station bench and used the knife's screwdriver on the screws on the bottom of the camper trailer toy. After Tyler took out a half dozen screws, the bottom of the little vehicle came off.

And Tyler pulled a baseball card out of the miniature trailer.

"That is Babe Ruth, isn't it?" Bill asked.

"The Babe, the Bambino, the Sultan of Slam," Tyler exclaimed. "One of the greatest players of all time. He's in a Boston Red Sox uniform! I'm guessing this card is worth thousands of dollars."

"Tyler!" said Madison. "How did you know it was inside, and how did the card get there?"

"You only looked at the outside of the camper trailer, to see what condition it was in," he said, "but I looked inside. I could just see part of the card at the bottom. I knew right away that I was looking at a Babe Ruth card because I'm a collector and I'd seen a poster of it at Stanley's store. Some kid must have valued the card a lot and hidden it in the toy to keep it safe."

"So are you going to sell it?" I asked.

"I don't know," Tyler said. "But I know I am one satisfied customer."

"At least," Madison said, "I'll be able to enjoy my birthday present now."

"You were right, Tyler," Bill said. "Most of the time, it's what's inside that matters."

Shockingly, this too is not an original story. The authorities at the National Association of Mystery Editors have compelled us to disclose the biblical origin of this final story. Can you guess?

☞ Turn to page 106 to find out!

The Case of the Fugitive Flyers

Q: *How did Bill know that Chris was telling stories and not the truth?*

A: Bill could tell Chris's story was a lie because of the stories Chris claimed he'd told. *Snow White* is a story written down by the Brothers Grimm. But Hans Christian Andersen wrote *The Little Mermaid*, not the Grimms. While the life of Pocahantas is often told in story form, Pocahantas was a historical person and not a fairy tale character.

Chris confessed that he had taken the flyers and thrown them away. He agreed to pay for the flyers and replace them at the places where he had stolen them.

Even though many flyers were thrown away by the people who got them, some flyers resulted in cases which appear in this very book.

The idea of finding truth in stories isn't original

with Bill. Jesus told stories all the time to teach truths about God, heaven and other important things.

Q: *This story isn't wholly original?*

A: This story comes in part from a story Jesus told. I know, you're thinking there were no warthog detectives in the Bible, but hear me out.

In the Bible, in Matthew, chapter 13 verses 3 to 8, Jesus told the story of a farmer who sowed seeds. Some of the seeds fell in rocks and weeds, some were eaten by birds, but some prospered.

The connection with the flyers is that some were ignored, some were stolen (Chris Franklin plays the role of the birds in this story), but some fulfilled their intended purpose of bringing in customers to Warthog Investigations.

I hope you can grow from truth you find in these stories.

The Case of the Sneezing Brother

Q: *Why were Mr. Henderson and Bill sure they knew which brother set up the croquet course?*

A: Bill needed to be positive which brother he should believe, though Caleb's allergies weighed in his favor. And Bill needed a way to prove to Mr. Henderson which brother was telling the truth.

Bill decided to use the rules of croquet to solve the case.

He asked the older brother Connor whether he used twelve wickets when setting up the course. Connor agreed that he had. Croquet uses nine wickets, not twelve.

Bill asked the younger brother Caleb whether he set up four stakes. Caleb corrected Bill and said he set up two. Two is the correct number of stakes according to the rules of croquet.

Mr. Henderson knew the croquet course was set up correctly, and he realized that Caleb was the only brother who could have done it. So he rewarded Caleb, and punished Connor for lying.

Q: *There are clues that this story is not original, so where does it come from?*

A: Jesus told a parable (found in Matthew 21:28-31) about two brothers. One said he would work in the vineyard, the other said he wouldn't. But the one who said he would, didn't. The one who said he would not, did.

Actions do speak louder than words – so act.

The Case of the Super Bowl Booth

Q: *How did Bill know that Chris, Tommy and Dwayne were lying?*

A: Because of the seasons. The Super Bowl is always at the end of January or, on very rare occasions, at the beginning of February.

The latest Tommy could go deer hunting is in December when the season ends. The NBA finals are in June, so Dwayne could not have tickets for that game on the same day as the Super Bowl. If the weather was cold enough for Nick's gloves and Bill's mittens, it certainly wouldn't be warm enough for Chris to go strawberry picking.

Bill knew they were lying to get out of what they thought would be a dull party at the Wilkersons' home.

Q: *I don't remember any football games in the*

Bible, so how could this be a Bible story?

A: Though there is no football in the Bible, there were parties. In Luke 14:15-24, Jesus tells the story of

a man who was throwing a large banquet. When he invited his friends to the banquet, they gave excuses.

"I have just bought a field."

"I just bought five yoke of oxen." (Have oxen ever kept you from a party?)

"I just got married."

Because these people turned down the invitation, the man invited the poor, the crippled, the blind and the lame, all the people who usually would get left out in those times.

Jesus was really talking about the kingdom of God. When He invites us to His party, we should not turn Him down.

Phil the Warthog and the Idle Jet Pack

Q: *The comic showed Lance making banana shakes instead of using the jet pack to take photographs high above the earth, but how could Shady know? Shady was away!*

A: I don't blame you if you didn't figure out the solution to this one. You would have to think logically and scientifically in a very illogical and unscientific setting.

Shady (and Bill) knew Lance could not have flown the jet pack as high as he said. Air gets thinner the higher you go in the air. People who climb Mt. Everest, all 28,000 feet of it, need to train for the difficulty they will have breathing and often need to use oxygen tanks. Airplanes, traveling at 40,000 feet, pressurize the cabins so people can breathe.

So Shady and Bill knew that Lance wouldn't have

been able to breathe if he had been traveling with the jet pack at 70,000 feet.

Q: *Nick said the story sounded familiar; why?*

A: There was a reason the story sounded familiar to Nick, and maybe to you.

Jesus told a parable (found in Matthew 25:14-30) about a master going on a trip who left his servants with different amounts of money. In the Bible story, the money was measured using a term called "talents," something like the way we measure money in the United States in dollars today. The master rewarded the two servants who used their talents profitably but threw out the third servant, who did not use his talent.

God has given us all different talents, abilities and stuff. What are you doing with what God has given you?

The Case of the Bogus Bowler

Q: *What evidence did Bill wish he could have used to bowl over Mr. Grumley?*

A: Bill didn't get to tell Mr. Grumley his evidence that Chris didn't know about bowling. The fact that Chris complained that Brian broke a rule when Chris had broken an even bigger rule was enough to get Brian into the Bowlathon.

Bill could have told Mr. Grumley that what Chris said had proved he didn't know about bowling scoring. If you make a strike, during your next turn the points you score on that frame carry back to the frame when you bowled a strike. So two strikes in a row are worth more than just twenty points.

In fact, a perfect game in bowling, with strikes in all ten frames (including strikes with each of the two remaining balls after the first strike in the tenth frame), would be 300 points because, you see, well . . . Anyway, Bill knew he could prove Chris didn't really know much about bowling.

Q: *Isn't the overall plot of this story strikingly familiar?*

A: Yes, this too is a story from the Bible.

In Matthew 18:23-24, Jesus told a story about a man who owed his master a huge debt. In our times, the debt would have been in the millions of dollars. The master forgave the debt.

Then the man forgiven for millions complained when he saw a friend who owed him a couple of bucks. This got the master really ticked off.

Jesus was teaching that God forgives us for all the rotten and stupid things we do, so we need to be willing to forgive others. Even little brothers, believe it or not.

Bill the Warthog Goes to the Dogs

Q: *How did Bill know that Mrs. Emily Thornton Bilencheck was trying a trick?*

A: Bill knew Mrs. Bilencheck was lying because of a suggestion she made: "Perhaps Nick's mother took the biscuits out of her purse."

Nick's mother's purse was with Nick's backpack and Bill's briefcase, yet Mrs. Bilencheck knew that the biscuits had been in the purse, not the briefcase or the backpack. Bill knew she had taken those dog treats.

Q: *What other story is in this story?*

A: If you look in the book of Matthew, in chapter 25, verses 1-13, you'll find that Jesus told a story about a wedding.

According to the traditions of the time, the bridesmaids would wait for the groom. They would wait with their lamps, and they needed oil to keep those lamps lit.

The bridesmaids would need burning lamps to join the wedding party. At this wedding, the groom  took a long time in coming. So five of the bridesmaids, the ones who didn't bring enough oil, weren't ready for the groom when he came.

Just like the bridesmaids in Jesus' story, half the trainers didn't bring enough dog biscuits and weren't ready for Max "Arf" Stevenson to come.

The Bible says Jesus is coming again, and we need to be ready for Him to come back.

Trust God to forgive your sins, keep praying and read the Bible. Always be ready so you won't run out of oil or biscuits.

The Case of the Stashed Treasure

Q: *Where be the treasure Seth found, me hearty?*

A: When Bill sat down, he thought about where the coin could be in an empty room. Then he realized the room wasn't empty. There was the flashlight.

Surely, they would check the flashlight to make sure it worked before such a competition. Unless the flashlight was there for another reason.

Bill told Seth to look for the coin inside the flashlight. Gold is not a good conductor of electricity, so even if the flashlight had batteries, the gold coin could keep it from working.

Seth found the coin in the flashlight.

Q: *What story from the Bible is pirated here?*

A: This is a fairly straight steal from the parable of Jesus found in Luke 15:8-10.

That parable is about a woman who had ten coins, lost one, searched for it, found it and rejoiced.

The point Jesus was making was that, if we are lost, God will look for us.

Imagine finding something you've missed greatly: a favorite toy, money, even a friend. No matter how happy you can imagine being about finding something you lost, God is even happier about being with you.

The Case of the Film Fake

Q: *Bill proved that Pauly lied on his application, but how?*

A: Mr. Lang hired Pauly because of his alleged expert knowledge of movies. Bill proved Pauly didn't really know much about film history.

Bill talked about the commanding voice of the actor who played Ben Hur in the 1925 version of the film, and Pauly agreed. The first "talkie," or film to include recorded dialog, was *The Jazz Singer* in 1927. That's two years later!

Now if you were thinking Bill could prove Pauly was a fake because films of that time were in black and white, you're close. The 1925 *Ben Hur* was one of the few films of the time that did use color; but only in twelve scenes, and not in the chariot scene.

Pauly had to admit he had never gone to film

school and had no right to hold Mr. Lang to his contract.

Q: *Is this story really a remake of an original?*

A: Yes, this story is a remake.

In Luke 16:1-9, Jesus told a most unusual story in which the hero is a dishonest guy. A money manager, who worked for a rich man, wasted the rich man's possessions. The manager was about to be fired.

The manager lowered the debts of everyone who owed the rich man money so that those people would approve of him.

Jesus said that in the same way, we need to realize that the stuff we have is on loan from a very rich guy (God), and we should make good use of it while we have it. And the best use of the things we have is to help other people.

 # The Case where Bill Goes Wild

Q: *How did Bill trap Eggleston into revealing himself as the poacher?*

A: Apparently, even in his dreams, Bill still thinks like a detective.

Bill could prove that Eggleston had never studied warthogs because if the man really was an expert on warthogs, he would have to know about the countries where warthogs live.

The United States of America is in the northern hemisphere. In the northern hemisphere, the cold months are December, January and February.

Eggleston assumed these would be the cold months in the country of South Africa, but that is not the case.

South Africa is in the southern hemisphere. In the southern hemisphere, the warm months are December,

January and February, with temperatures the same as those during summer in the northern hemisphere.

Q: *Is there a story like this in the Bible?*

A: In Luke 18:1-8, you can find a story Jesus told about a widow who pleads with an evil judge to give

 her justice from her enemy. The judge finally does what she asks because she bothers him so persistently.

If even rotten or lazy people like the judge or the game ranger will help when they are asked repeatedly, Jesus taught, then surely our good Father God will help us if we ask Him.

So, when you are in need, don't forget to ask God. He wants to help.

The Case
of the
Unwanted Gift

Q: *Was Tyler so sure the toy was worth buying because he'd read a similar story?*

A: The case of the unwanted gift is the last story, and once again we must admit that it is not totally original.

Jesus told a story, found in Matthew 13:44, about a man who found a treasure in a field.

The man knew the treasure was worth a lot, more than anything he owned. Obviously, he didn't let on to anyone that there was treasure in the field, or he would have lost the chance to get it for himself. So he sold all he had, to buy the field and to get the treasure as well.

This chapter echoes the story of Jesus. Tyler sold everything he owned to buy the toy because he was a trading card collector and he knew the treasure inside the toy (the Babe Ruth card) was worth more than everything he owned.

As with all His parables, Jesus told the story of the treasure in the field to make a point. He said the treasure was the kingdom of heaven, which was worth more than anything. We can be a part of God's kingdom if we trust in Jesus to forgive our sins and enter our life.

What's even cooler is that this is a treasure we don't have to keep secret. God wants us to share this treasure with everyone. And this treasure is yours for the asking.

So what's keeping you? Ask God for the treasure of His kingdom. It's the deal none of us can afford to pass up.

"Crime is like a cockroach, but not as tasty."

– Bill the Warthog

Get more Bill with *Full Metal Trench Coat*, the first book in the **Bill the Warthog Mysteries** series. Can you solve the crimes for Nick and his friends before Bill does?

ISBN 10: 1-58411-068-6
ISBN 13: 978-1-58411-068-2